We Live Without a Future

and other stories by Julie Bozza

LIBRAtiger

Published by LIBRAtiger 2025

ISBN: 978-1-925869-40-8

"In Fair Verona" and "In a Dark House" previously published in *No Holds Bard*, Fiona Pickles (editor), Manifold Press, 2018.
"Verity" previously published in *Clarity*, Other Worlds Ink, 2022.
"Magic Casements" previously published in *Queer Weird West Tales*, Julie Bozza (editor), LIBRAtiger, 2022.
"Chooser of the Slain" previously published in *Heroines, Volume 2*, Sarah Nicholson and Caitlin White (editors), The Neo Perennial Press, 2019.
"We Live Without a Future" previously published in *Call to Arms*, Heloise Mezen (editor), Manifold Press, 2017.

juliebozza.com

Table of Contents

◆

Sunday, 26 January 1941

A battle against depression, rejection ... This trough of despair shall not, I swear, engulf me. ...

There's a lull in the war. Six nights without raids. But Garvin says the greatest struggle is about to come ... It's the cold hour, this: before the lights go up. A few snowdrops in the garden. Yes, I was thinking: **we live without a future.** *That's what's queer: with our noses pressed to a closed door.*

Friday, 7 February 1941

Why was I depressed? I cannot remember.

Virginia Woolf, *A Writer's Diary*

In Fair Verona

♦

George Gordon Byron, the 6th Baron Byron, arrived in Verona with his people and his baggage, and deigned to stay for a night – or for two at the most. As his servant, William Fletcher, laboriously negotiated the rent for a suite of rooms in an old palazzo to which they had been directed, Byron strolled over to a vantage point and considered the town. Verona seemed entirely unexceptional, huddled either side of a broad sweep of river. Byron suspected that the poets had lyricised more on Verona than Verona had really deserved.

Eventually Fletcher approached and indicated that they had arranged for rooms and beds enough for comfort. "My lord," he added, "the signore suggests you might stay for the two nights, and visit the tomb of the Capulets tomorrow."

Byron stared in disdainful surprise, and Fletcher bore it as stoically as he always did. "Good God, man," Byron eventually responded, "the Capulets of renown are to be found in a play, a poem, a story – never in history."

Fletcher took a moment, and concluded, "So, no tombs, then?"

"Just so. Tell the signore one night, and we'll decide in the morning on the rest. It might be amusing, after all, to hear the fancies spun by a guide."

The palazzo itself was a fine old building of pale stone, repaired in places with red brick. Inside there was to be found a dusty kind of luxury. Byron let Fletcher and the others organise the rooms, only claiming a book-lined parlour as his own. His habit was to stay up late to write after everyone else had gone to bed, and this room with its neglected library and its view over red-tiled rooftops to an indistinct horizon suited his current mood.

The palazzo, he heard over a late supper, dated back to the early fifteenth century – so Byron was unsurprised that night, after his household and the town itself had settled into sleep, when he was visited by an apparition.

A man as transparent as gauze appeared before him, as if he'd just walked into the room through the heavily burdened bookshelves. He had a tumble of thick unruly curls, perhaps russet in colour, and a cynical curl to his upper lip. The lower lip, though, was full and lush and put Byron in mind of joys he had not tasted for far too long.

The apparition drew near, stepping with a suppleness that showed off the gracefulness of his long, stockinged legs, and moving across the floor perhaps a little faster than his gait warranted. But who cared for that, when there were such limbs to admire? Byron's gaze travelled appreciatively upwards, past the padded hose and the slightly shabby doublet, to the expression of nonchalant curiosity. Ghosts weren't so unexpected, Byron supposed, in a place such as this, but he would never have imagined a ghost coming forward to lean elegantly over his writing desk and consider the papers strewn there.

Byron had been trying to start a new poem on the subject of a love tragically forbidden by the Doge of Venice and ending in the peaceful green depths of the lagoon – but his words so far were scrawled without reason or rhythm, as he had yet to find the correct metre for the thing.

Accordingly, the apparition seemed unimpressed as he straightened to his full height again, though his eyes – bright, intelligent, and the sharpest thing about him – now considered Byron himself with the same curiosity. "Ah," the apparition said in a dry whisper, "yet another scribbler."

The words and, for that matter, the cadence were English. Byron frowned in confusion, but promptly answered, "Yes." Then he bridled at the dismissive tone. He knew well enough that his own doubts and false starts that night were only temporary. "I am a poet. And you, sir?"

"Oh, I am *composed* of words, sir. I was conjured into being by a poet."

"You were made of words?" Byron echoed.

"I am nothing *but* words. Clever ones, true, but nothing more."

While touring old Europe, Byron had been quite prepared to encounter the restless souls of those long-dead. This should have been a ghost, in all the ways that Byron understood such things to work. He was insubstantial, so that Byron could see through the apparition to the candlelight glinting off the gilt lettering on the books' spines. But he was also real, for his clothes were no fancy dress costume, his face was not painted, and he carried no theatrical properties.

Byron ventured, "You were not once flesh?"

"No, I was ink on parchment, and words on men's lips. I still am, for that matter. I am conjured and conjured again... There is no rest for one such as me."

Byron stared at the apparition, feeling somewhat affronted. "That's a pretty conceit," he said after a while. "Then perhaps you are acquainted with my Harold, or my Conrad, or my Bonivard? Can you summon *them* to meet their Creator?"

The cynical curl grew more pronounced, and the apparition's tone was disdainful. "There are few like me. It is a rare love that brought me into being. A rare love of the most passionate kind – and a rare hatred, too, just as passionate. Had you written any such, you would know."

Byron was afire with the possibilities. He thought of Marlowe conjuring Mephistopheles in words, and Byron knew that he, too, could create such a creature. He pushed away the scrawled papers, and reached for a fresh sheet. "Spirit," he demanded, "tell me your name."

There was only laughter in response, and the form faded away as if a light air had drawn it back into the books. Byron paid no further attention, but dipped his pen in ink and quickly flew out a verse from his fingertips. It was in iambic pentameter. Sometimes the obvious choices were the best. It was the rhythm of a man's walk. Of a man's heartbeat.

He shrugged off the shawl he'd worn for

warmth, and wrote until the edge of the sky began to pale. Then, as a few distant hints of reawakening life began to sound clear through the crispness of pre-dawn, Byron flung down his pen, and stalked to his rooms.

Fletcher always slept in Byron's dressing room – or at the foot of his bed, or in the next room along, depending on their accommodations – for he was still Byron's valet, although also organiser of Byron's roving household, complainer-in-chief, and more besides. Byron leaned down to the cot to shake Fletcher's sturdy shoulder, and Fletcher blinked awake.

"Come," said Byron, standing again and stepping towards his bedroom. "Come."

Fletcher blinked once more and then a smile broadened his aging yet still handsome face. "The poetising is going well, then, my lord?" he asked, purely rhetorically, as he padded along in Byron's wake. "It's been too long since you last had need of me."

"We'll stay in Verona for a few nights, perhaps," Byron responded, not entirely inconsequentially.

"As you wish, my lord." A moment later, Fletcher was kneeling on the floor by Byron's bed, and Byron slipped in between, unbuttoning his britches and then leaning back against the edge of the mattress. Fletcher yawned hugely, like a lion, shook his golden-grey curls – and, not bothering to shut his mouth again, he pounced and swallowed Byron whole.

◆

The next night, Byron wrote and wrote until his hand cramped and his inkwell ran dry, heedless of the uneasy sense of wariness that lingered by the books in the parlour. Heedless of it, or driven by it, actually he could not say. He only knew that he must write – until dawn glimmered and peace returned to the room. That marked enough. Byron threw down his pen, and went to fetch Fletcher.

"I'll need ink, man," Byron said as they walked to his bed. "Buy me ink today, and more paper, too."

"Yes, my lord. And in the meantime, you need...?"

"Oh yes, I *do* need." And they were far too familiar with each other by now for either to have to spell it out.

◆

On another midnight, Byron puzzled over his new verses, casting about from sheet to sheet as if the meaning would come clear if only he could find the right order in which to place them. "These make no sense!" he muttered at last, pushing them all away.

"Yet you cast quite a spell," the apparition said – startling Byron, as another visitation had been wished for but not counted upon. "For what is a spell but words?"

Byron sat back in the chair and considered the fellow. They were of an age, he thought, as near as he could tell. The apparition looked to be not yet thirty, and Byron was twenty-eight. Presumably that was how the apparition had been written. An aeon could have passed since then, of course. No, Byron corrected himself; judging by the spirit's clothes, it had been perhaps two or three hundred years. And was there something about the doublet and hose that hinted more of England than Italy? Just as the spirit spoke in a proper English, if slightly antiquated. It all made for a fine puzzle.

"Tell me your name," Byron commanded.

The apparition gave him a mocking bow. "I warrant you could guess. I will not say it. With every iteration of my name, my sentence grows longer, and I linger here caught between all worlds and none."

"I shall guess, then," Byron agreed. "You spoke of a love most passionate?"

"I did indeed. I loved a man –"

"Ah!" That was a choice clue.

The apparition cast him a wry look. "I loved a man truly – and my tragedy was that he loved a woman just as truly."

"That does not narrow it down," Byron complained.

"No. But I also hated – as fiercely as I loved. I hated her dearest cousin. Really, I despised the man."

The shape of that found an answering echo in Byron's mind.

"Between the three of them, they killed me. Ah, none of them quite meant to do so. But our tangled fate was inexorably set in motion when my love met his love... and I died cursing him." The spirit stared bleakly into the past of his own story, and whispered again, "I died cursing him and her and all their people, may God forgive me."

Byron nodded. "You were not Marlowe's, then, you are not Mephistopheles, but another M."

The apparition nodded, and held out a hand as if to prevent further words –

– but Byron was already uttering, "Mercutio."

Another nod, and the form became slightly more substantial. Nearer muslin than gauze now. The spirit sighed.

Byron sighed, too, in satisfaction.

Of a sudden, his new verses made sense, and he turned to them, reshuffled the papers, and he *knew*. It all came clear in his mind. "I will write of you," he said – though when he looked up, the spirit had gone again. It hardly mattered. Byron's pen danced as fast as ink-stained fingers could drive it.

He was still writing at dawn, when Fletcher brought a pot of coffee, and Byron paused for a quickly snatched kiss – fond on Fletcher's part and passionate though distracted on Byron's. Then he began writing once more.

◆

"What of your love?" Byron asked on another midnight. "What of Romeo?"

The spirit winced but did not sour. "He is at peace. He and his love found each other in the places beyond words, and drifted together into peace. They are as happy as anyone can be."

"But Tybalt must still be as restless as you are?"

"No. No, he paid his price, and justice let him find oblivion."

"It is only you, then, left to haunt me...?"

Mercutio nodded, his reddish-brown curls tossing fantastically, and his eerily light eyes glinting with a hint of green. He really was beautiful. Shakespeare himself must have imagined Mercutio exactly thus. Had that poet felt this same attraction? How could he not? And surely that, too, had something to do with Mercutio's continuance.

"I will write of you," Byron promised.

"It will help neither you nor me."

"I will write you into a fuller life."

Mercutio stared at him with a sardonic kind of wonder.

"Not that I presume –" Byron broke off, before adding with scrupulous honesty, "Well, maybe I presume a little – to follow in the footsteps of your Creator. To build further on what he has achieved."

"Oh my lord," Mercutio whispered dryly, and then on another sigh he was gone, fading back into the overfull bookshelves.

Byron reached for the ink and took up the tale, which had been evanescent until now when the story began to firm into the gentle colours of a sunrise.

What man, after all, did not want a demon lover to call his own? Marlowe had had his Mephistopheles, and if Shakespeare had not been wise enough to keep Mercutio tethered closely enough for himself alone to enjoy, then Byron would not make the same mistake.

"Fletcher," he demanded later, in the pre-dawn coolness. "Come to bed."

"Aye, sir," the man obligingly agreed, stumbling after Byron still half asleep. "I do like it when he's writing," Fletcher mumbled to himself, as if still dreaming.

Byron turned, grabbed his shoulders and shook him fully awake. "Ravish me, man. Ravish me as you were wont to do in the hay of the stables." Oh, *those* had been the days, back home in Newstead, when the world was young and fresh and full of endless possibilities.

"*Aye*, sir," was the happy reply, as if in this moment Fletcher felt the world was ever thus.

◆

On the seventh night, Mercutio seemed almost substantial enough for Byron to kiss – to kiss and to keep for himself for ever. Byron stood leaning on the mantelpiece watching the firelight shift and gleam on the dark purple velvet of Mercutio's clothes, while Mercutio read through the poem, wafting each finished page away across the desk with a breath or a flutter of his fingers.

Byron watched, not impatiently at all, but admiring, enthralled. This would be love as it should be – passionate, and returned like for like. Not a hopeless love for a man who loved another, as Mercutio had known. Not a too-pure love destroyed by an imposed distance and an untimely death, as Byron had suffered. This would be a love fully acknowledged, engaged and eternal.

Mercutio looked up, his face alight although also... wistful, perhaps even sad. There was much of significance to contemplate, after all. They were both silent for long moments, in anticipation of all they would share, in the present, in the years to come, and then beyond words, beyond life.

Eventually Mercutio said, "This is very good. No, this is excellent."

It was the simple truth. Byron nodded. He could not deny the truth to the poem's source of inspiration.

"It is exquisite. Ephemeral and earthy, both at once. How did you do it?" Mercutio shook his head as if in disbelief. His hair moved now just like a real man's would. Anyone walking past the open doorway and glancing in would assume he was a neighbour, a visitor, a friend. A lover.

"With such a Muse," Byron offered, gesturing at Mercutio with unfamiliar humility.

Mercutio sat back in the chair, letting it support his weight, and considered Byron cautiously.

"Please," Byron stuttered, like the clumsy schoolboy he'd been when he first felt real love. "Please. May I kiss you?"

A moment stretched and then Mercutio seemed to soften a little towards him. As a flesh-and-blood man would soften when he had finally resolved within himself what needed doing. "Yes," Mercutio said. "Yes, you may kiss me. If I may ask a favour in turn."

"Anything," Byron promised.

"You will not like it."

"Anything," he vowed again, for a gentleman kept his word no matter what it cost him. Or was it possible that –?

"Destroy it," Mercutio asked. He gestured towards the papers spread across the desk to ensure his meaning was clear. "This poem is a thing of great beauty, my lord. But I ask you to put it in the fire and set it loose from your memory."

Byron just stared at him. This poem would be the making of him as a poet. Would – would have been, quite literally, the making of the two of them as lovers.

"You have written me into this world," Mercutio was continuing, gentle but relentless. "No one else could have achieved it. And so you alone have the means to free me."

"But I want –" Byron started. He was not unaware of the enormity of what Mercutio asked. Of how such a thing far outweighed what Byron himself craved. Yet he stuttered out, "A kiss. You promised – a kiss."

"I did so promise." Mercutio rose and slowly stepped towards him. Stepped towards him properly, with his feet meeting the floor. He was a man, oh, such a man. He was perfection. The Bard had surpassed himself. And was Byron really expected to give this up? Perhaps, he thought wildly, the kiss would be so wonderful that Mercutio would no longer wish for peace but instead yearn for life and love. Perhaps –

Mercutio was close now, scented with old books and new blood. Byron could almost hear the man's heartbeat. Their lips met, and Mercutio's mouth was cool though his kiss was hot with passion. He was clever and hungry and generous and demanding all at once – everything one could ask for from a lover.

And Byron knew even as he lost himself in the pleasure of it, he knew he must do as Mercutio wished.

When Mercutio pressed his mouth hard against him once more and then withdrew, Byron closed his eyes tighter still and reached blindly for the papers. Gathered up his most perfect poem, and turned with a wrenching sob to cast it into the flames. He watched, then, as the papers crackled and swiftly turned to pure black fragments which rose and danced in the warmth until finally they flew heavenward through the chimney.

One last sigh brushed across his ear, his cheek. "My lord..." came the whisper. "My love."

Byron was alone again, and would be for aye.

After a while he took up a shawl, wrapped it around his shoulders for what warmth it might give, and settled into the chair. He would let Fletcher have his rest for once, he would let the man wake naturally.

Byron wondered if he himself would ever truly rest again.

◆

Verity

◆

Her mind was clear, but the rest of her barely existed at all; she was translucent at best, when in life she'd been bold enough to write her own indelible truths. Of course, by the time her pen's ink on paper became printer's ink within books, these truths were somewhat diluted...

So, she should be used to it, really. She shouldn't be surprised to see her darling Stella described as her "boon companion" or her "bosom friend", or her pious "helpmeet". Even the latest biography, which claimed to be daring, settled for "life partner" – and then skated over the full implications with an "Of course we can't *know*...". Daring, indeed!

And she couldn't do anything about it. Black ink on white paper might prove fragile in the living world; might be ephemeral, hidden, or obscured. But for her the marks made were solid and immutable.

Until eventually an age dawned in which her Stella-star could have become her lawfully wedded wife. Among other such wonders was an encyclopedia composed entirely of light and electricity... And after some experimentation on these newfangled pixels, she discovered that at last she could actually *do* something.

Slowly, one by one, readers awoke to see the words "her love, her lover, Stella" and some even followed the reference to "manuscripts in trunk, Thornleigh Park attic". A few climbed into their motor vehicles and embarked on a treasure hunt. Excited chatter arose in hearts, in person, in print, in pixels...

The next biography, and the ones after that, she knew, would finally be founded in fact. Which meant that maybe it was time to move on, and join again with Stella's soul... and find peace.

◆

In a Dark House

◆

The mule was stubborn. But for now she wanted to go in much the same direction as did Feste, and so he let her have her way. He must ride, for he had been born lame, with both legs curved outwards in a bow – not that anyone could tell, when he was astride a mount. Feste must ride, for he couldn't walk far, though he could dance and tumble with the best of them, and had learned to make both beauty and farce of his rolling gait.

While the mule and he climbed up through the forest, Feste felt somewhat sheltered from the cold. He had a bag slung over his back round one shoulder, and his lute slung round the other, and they pressed against him, preserving what little warmth he had. The evergreen trees pushed close to the winding path, their dry buds starting to swell into fresh new life. But as the sun reached its zenith, still low in the late-winter sky, Feste and the mule abruptly emerged through the tree line. The barren slopes towered dizzyingly above – and the cold, and the glare of the pale stone, slammed into Feste almost taking his breath away. The mule seemed oblivious, though, and plodded on up the path as if she had business ahead that could not be ignored. Feste lowered his gaze, wrapped his arms around himself, and hunkered in for the duration.

Eventually, as the sun began casting their

shadow far ahead of them, a wedge of darkening sky darted down towards the mountain pass, and a dark-timbered building showed hard against the white-gold stone. It must be the inn he had been told of, on the edges of what he knew, where Illyria ended and some other country began. "We'll stop there for the night, shall we?" Feste said to the mule. He was in dire need of warmth and wine and victuals, so he prepared himself to tumble off his perch – without landing atop his lute and smashing it – if she decided for whatever reason to just keep going. But at the last moment, she turned off the path, and came to a halt near the stables.

"Good," said Feste, patting her shoulder appreciatively, before gathering himself to dismount – an inevitably untidy proceeding, even when he wasn't stiff and sore after a long day. By the time he had straightened up as much as he ever could, and climbed the few steps up to the terrace, a man in a leather apron had come to the door.

"Welcome, master traveller," the man said, shifting the empty platter he carried under one arm so he could swing the door open wide with the other. "Come in, and tell me what you need."

Feste sketched a grin. "Why, that could be a long list, sir, but for now I will trouble you only for provisions and a place to sleep, for this night at least."

With the smoothest tact, the innkeeper offered, "We have a small room on this floor, or a larger room above...?"

"The small room, I thank you."

"As you will, sir."

As Feste followed the man down a dim hallway, he asked, "And my fellow traveller, the mule?"

"She shall also be made welcome, sir."

"Good."

"Shall we charge her separately for what she requires?"

Feste cast the man a dry look as he was ushered past into a room that was indeed small but contained the necessities. "Ah, a wit! It is just as well you have yours about you, for mine have failed. No, sir," he continued heavily, "charge the woman's bed and board to me."

"As you will. My name is Bato, when you have need of me." The innkeeper withdrew with a respectful nod, and shut the door behind him.

Once he was alone, Feste heeled off his shoes, shrugged off his baggage, and stretched out on the bed – flat on his back and as tall as he could – and revelled in the comfort. Only that morning, having quickly become reacquainted with the luxuries of the Countess Olivia's house, Feste would have thought this mattress a poor thing. Now, after hours on the road on a mule with no saddle, he thought it as much of heaven as he would ever know.

Feste wasn't aware of falling into a doze, but when a bell was rung twice, he startled awake. That must be the sign that supper was about to be served in the main room. The bedroom was drowsy with twilight, but Feste could see well enough, and he had a hunger that was almost painful. He scrambled to sit up, to push his feet into his shoes, and then he hobbled down the hallway just as fast as he may.

"Fool!"

Feste was looking about him for the best seat, near the fire but not too near, convenient to be waited upon yet not in the way of all the anticipated comings and goings.

"Fool!"

He startled again, and Feste looked about him for something familiar. Someone known to him.

"FOOL! What do you do here?"

And it was Malvolio towering over him, of course, dressed in black and with a furious expression to match – and Feste smiled, for he had already found what he was looking for.

"Are you playing truant from my lady's house *again*? Barely three moons have waned since you returned from your last jaunt."

Feste considered him with a sharp eye. "What would you care if I were? You swore you hated the lot of them."

Malvolio glared down at him. "And you as well," he ground out.

"And you hate me, too, that's so," Feste easily agreed.

Malvolio sagged a little, and turned to go back to his seat. Feste followed him, though he knew he'd hardly be welcome, and sat at the next table along from Malvolio.

They were both silent for a while, each staring ahead as if alone. Bato brought Feste a jug of dark wine and a goblet, and Feste toasted both Bato and Malvolio before drinking. The wine was raw and refreshing, and seemed to scour clean both throat and head.

"Fool, what are you doing here?" Malvolio eventually asked in somewhat quieter tones.

"I came to find you."

Malvolio cast him a scowling look. "You mock me. I should know better than to expect anything else."

"It is the truth. This night you'll have nothing but truth from me."

"Why?" Malvolio demanded.

"Why did I look for you? I wanted to tell you something. No," Feste corrected himself, for he had indeed promised himself to be as honest as this wine. He took another mouthful before saying, "I wanted to ask something of you."

Malvolio had half-turned in his seat to consider him. Curiosity, reluctance and doubt battled across his face. Eventually he prompted, "What, then?"

Another pause dragged by. Bato brought them each a bowl of stew and a share of bread. They both ignored the food for now. Feste said, "Those we left behind – the Countess Olivia and her household, and her friends at the Count Orsino's house –"

"Yes?"

"You vowed revenge upon them."

Malvolio turned away again, his scowl returned in full measure. "I did, and with reason."

Feste leaned towards him, offering or inviting a confidence. "I would ask you –"

"And I vowed revenge upon you among the pack," Malvolio reminded him.

"I would ask you to leave them be."

Malvolio's glance skewered him. "Why?"

Feste tore off a chunk of bread, and dipped it in the stew before eating it. The food was as blunt and hearty as the wine. He took up his spoon, and helped himself to another mouthful. After a while he said, as if inconsequentially, "They are all happy now. All paired up and absorbed in love."

"What is that to me?" Malvolio stirred at his stew so vigorously it almost spattered across the table. "Why should they be happy and treat me so miserably?"

"Leave them be," Feste said again. "Do not grudge them something that you or I may never find."

Malvolio glared at him. "You think I should leave you be, too, I suppose – though it was your Sir Topas who dealt the killing blow."

Feste swallowed a retort, and hung his head. It was shameful that he had finally given himself over to Maria and Sir Toby's game against Malvolio, and pretended to be the curate come to comfort him in his confinement. And yet all Malvolio's previous taunts and harsh words against the fool were still sharp in Feste's mind. "I had reason enough to dislike you," he muttered.

But then, before Malvolio could respond to this, Feste turned towards him and said, "I only ask you to leave them be – I do not ask for my sake. You can do what you will with me."

A suspicious glare, and then Malvolio returned his attention to his food and his own thoughts, as if unsure what to make of this or how best to respond.

The two of them ate in silence for a while. It

seemed there were only a handful of other travellers at the inn, all gathered around a table in the far corner, talking familiarly and sharing banter as if they knew each other well. Malvolio and Feste were ignored by all but Bato, who served them with quiet attention.

At last, though, when they were done eating, Bato approached and asked, "Was that a lute you brought with you, sir? Would you favour us with a song?"

Feste sighed, but he answered, "It was and I will – if you, kind sir, will save me the trouble and fetch it from my room."

The choice of tune was an obvious one:

When that I was and a little tiny boy,
With hey, ho, the wind and the rain,
A foolish thing was but a toy,
For the rain it raineth every day.

Malvolio hadn't heard the song the last time Feste sang it – and he didn't hear much of it this time, either, for by the time Feste was into the third verse, Malvolio had walked away. His heavy footsteps could be heard going up the wooden stairs, determinedly clumping out of time with the music.

Feste sighed. And then he switched to more cheerful fare, which at least earned him more wine.

◆

The next morning, after he had broken his

fast, Feste ambled out into the crisp clear day. The mountain air tasted sharp, almost metallic. It made him feel both giddy and focused.

When Feste saw that Malvolio was sitting on a bench on the terrace, he walked over, and sat nearby. His nodded greeting was ignored, and so they remained silent for a time, each staring out across the prospect. To their left, far below, lay the green undulations and distant mists of Illyria; above and to their right, the dry narrow pass that led elsewhere. The future was before them, in one direction or the other.

Eventually, Malvolio cautiously ventured, "When you said that they were all paired up... My lady could not have accepted that drunken friend of Sir Toby's, I trust."

"Sir Andrew?" Feste mused for long moments. Which wasn't entirely about aggravating Malvolio's anxiety. Feste hadn't expected that Malvolio himself would provide a conversational lead into Feste's subject. "No," Feste said at last. "Sir Andrew was abandoned, cast adrift, just as we were."

"You?" Malvolio harrumphed. "I am sure that if you deigned to stay and be loyal, you'd be welcomed as warmly as ever. But you are too restless! Too unsettled!"

"It is true," Feste acknowledged in halting tones, "that since the old master died, I have not cared to stay. It is the same place, and much the same people, and yet everything has changed."

"My lady loves you as well as her father ever did, though God only knows why."

"Perhaps not *quite* so well." Feste cast an

uneasy glance at Malvolio. Of course Malvolio wasn't going to make this easy for him. But now the steward was encouraging Feste to return to the Countess Olivia's household? Surely not! Or did Feste's presence matter less in Malvolio's absence?

Feste cleared his throat before asking, "How long have you been here? Have you been in this place ever since you left?"

Malvolio drew himself up into his usual stern stance, and did not answer.

"Why have you not gone any further?" Feste persisted. In truth, it had only been a handful of days – but Malvolio could have been far beyond Feste's reach by now. It should have been nigh on impossible to find him.

Perhaps Malvolio was ruminating on a similar question, for he finally grated out, "But why did you follow me?" He sounded thoroughly baffled, as if it were the last thing he had expected.

"I did not care to follow Sir Andrew," Feste replied.

A slight twitch of one shoulder indicated that Malvolio could acknowledge that as a fair argument.

"I might have chosen to follow Antonio, a man of my own nature."

"A fool, then?"

"Love makes fools of us all, that much is clear. No, he was another man thrown off unwanted..." Feste paused for a moment's consideration. "Much happened while you were confined. Our lady Olivia loved the Count Orsino's man Cesario – perhaps you had a glimpse of that, at least. But she married

Cesario's twin brother Sebastian, thinking they were one man and not two."

Malvolio cried brokenly, "My lady is married?"

Feste cast him a look of soft sorrow and fellow feeling. "Love makes fools of us all," he repeated. "You were wrong to place your hopes in her, my friend."

"I am not your friend," Malvolio stiffly replied.

"Well, then. The count had also loved Cesario, in his way, so when Cesario was revealed to be a lady in disguise, he offered for her hand."

Malvolio was all astonishment.

"It is true. Viola and Sebastian of Messaline, cast on Illyria's shores by a shipwreck, and none to tell them apart when they were in the same garb."

After long moments, Malvolio dared to ask, "Will it be well with my lady? With this Sebastian...?"

"If he is as like to his sister in temperament as in looks, then she has as good a chance as any at happiness."

Malvolio nodded, and then was obliging enough to pick up the earlier thread of conversation. "So, this Antonio was...?"

"A friend and companion to Sebastian, though he wished for more." Feste sighed. "Love, as I may have already observed –"

"Yes," said Malvolio, cutting him off.

Feste rolled his head around, easing the tension in his neck and shoulders. "I might have followed him," he quietly continued at last. "I might have sought comfort, both freely given and received. But instead I came to you."

"You chose wrong. I want nothing from you."

"Not revenge?"

"Of my own," Malvolio averred. "Not of your doing."

"Well, then," Feste concluded.

Malvolio said nothing more, but stood and walked inside the house.

◆

After the midday meal, Feste visited the mule, and made sure she was fed and watered. Which of course she was, and it wasn't that Feste didn't trust Bato to take good care of all his guests. She seemed content, and certainly more willing to listen to Feste's ruminations than Malvolio had been.

Though Feste found himself rambling to a verbal halt in short order. "I wonder now why I did follow him," Feste confided. "What did I think I could say to him that would shed any light on the matter?" He paused for a long while, pondering that, before concluding, "I really wonder, to be honest, what exactly is the matter in question."

The mule stared at him blankly, and then returned her attention to her provision of hay.

Malvolio himself appeared a moment later, stalking into the stables in high dudgeon. "What did you mean?" he hissed at Feste, apparently trying for discretion despite overwhelming anger. "Why tell me of this unnatural... lust of that man's? Of *yours*?"

Feste sighed. "You can do with me what you will."

"I want nothing from you!"

"Then take nothing, do nothing. But listen to me while I tell you the truth. That is all I know to do. It is up to you what happens then."

"If you think that I share this –"

"I know you do not," said Feste. "I know what your feelings have been for our lady Olivia. I honour you for the truth at the heart of those feelings."

Malvolio took a step back, a little shocked at first. And then he seemed reluctantly appeased, in some small measure. Finally a hint of shame painted his sallow cheeks a slightly healthier pink.

"Do only this for me," Feste said again, in the most reasonable tones. "Listen to me. Listen – and if it makes no difference, I will leave. Alone. I expect nothing."

"Well, then," said Malvolio. And he lifted an arm with an odd kind of grace towards the inn, inviting Feste to join him there.

It was a beginning at last.

◆

The raw dark wine helped them take the next step. Or helped Feste, at least. They sat in the cool darkness of the main room, where the fire had not yet been brought back to life. The other travellers had left on the next stage of their journey, and once Bato had left the wine he discreetly absented himself. And so while Feste spoke in low tones, he spoke clear.

"Love comes to me in many forms, but lust only ever in the shape of a man."

Malvolio stared at him, waiting for more, his face cool but expectant. Eventually, when Feste didn't continue, Malvolio said, "But why do you think I care to know? It has naught to do with me."

"You can do with me what you will," Feste repeated.

Malvolio's face contorted as if an apoplexy threatened.

"You swore revenge," Feste reminded him. "Leave them be, and use me for the purpose. Resent me, report me, abuse me – whatever you will."

At last Malvolio's attention was focussed fully on Feste. He appeared to be an entirely different man when he wasn't thinking only of himself. Feste felt a spark of hope.

"Report me as an unnatural creature. I'll not deny it. I have nothing left to lose, and the man I loved best of all is dead, so he'll come to no harm." Feste shrugged, and said directly, "Have me locked away in darkness, just as you were. Will that answer?"

Malvolio had lifted a hand to stop the spill of words. "Enough. I understand."

"I am tired of pretence," Feste found himself confessing. "If it must be truth or freedom, then I choose truth."

"And so there will be no more of your quibbling sophistications over words?"

Feste laughed under his breath. "Yet I had thought even my quibbles were about clarity."

Malvolio cast him a dry look, and did not

deign to comment.

After a silence had swelled and then eased between them, Feste prompted, "Well? What are you thinking?"

"I am thinking that I do not forgive you for Sir Topas," Malvolio declared – before proceeding in more cautious tones, "but it was you who brought me pen and paper, and light to see by. Writing that letter to my lady led to my freedom. And so... perhaps... your account has already been balanced. Fool," he added, as if he must.

Feste huffed a laugh. "Revenge always hits wide of its mark, but I am not an arbitrary target."

"No," said Malvolio, decisively. "Not you."

"But the others...?" he persisted. "You may find, my friend, the idea of revenge will taste sweet to you now, but the fact of it will be sour."

"Enough!" Malvolio cried – and then he groaned in frustration. "Why do you care so much? Do they care for you any more than for me? What do you owe them?"

Well. He had promised to be entirely honest. Feste swallowed past the barrier in his throat, and spoke one half of the truth. "For the sake of the old man whom I loved dearer than any in all the world, I would have his daughter be left to her happiness."

No one had heard that from him before, save the one most nearly concerned.

Malvolio stared at him sharply askance, and then – finally – nodded. But all he said was, "We shall see."

And Feste thought that he could ask no more.

◆

Feste packed up his few belongings in the cool brightness of the following morning, and settled his account with Bato. He slung his bag across his back over one shoulder, and his lute over the other. When he walked outside, with a rolling gait to accommodate the night's chill that had not yet relinquished its hold on his hips, Feste saw that the mule was waiting for him. She was facing towards the mountain pass that led into another country.

"Good," said Feste, patting her shoulder. She stood patiently while he clambered onto her back, though he had to clutch hard at her to be sure he wouldn't fall before he settled. "Good," he said once more when he was ready.

She set off at an easy pace – and a figure fell into step beside them. Feste looked up at the silhouette dark against the sun, and then squinted as the figure took another pace forward and the light fell full upon him again. It was Malvolio, of course.

"If you can bear a companion," Malvolio said, with a rare hint of diffidence. After a moment he met Feste's gaze, before his glance dropped away.

"I'm not going back," Feste warned him.

"I would think not."

The inn was already falling behind them, and the sky was a deep rich blue just beyond the sharp crest of the pass.

"Then," said Feste, "together we shall see what lies beyond Illyria, my friend."

"I am not your friend," Malvolio responded, in tones that were now more weary than outraged.

Feste grinned up at him, and winked. "Good," he said. And on they travelled, at a mule's stubborn pace, into the new day.

◆

Magic Casements

◆

This brand-new town of Leadville, Colorado, barely old enough to be breeched, felt raw and tawdry to Oscar Wilde. The farther west he travelled in the United States of America, the more it was so – despite Leadville's Tabor Grand Opera House with its gilt and velvet, where he would lecture that evening.

Once Oscar had acclimated himself to the country, however, he'd begun to find the place fascinating. Invigorating, even. Not least due to its astonishing myriad of people.

The miners of Leadville, in particular, seemed to comprise anyone capable of the work – men and occasional women of all shades and styles, of all creeds and countries – including a young man with an accent approximating French who had taken quite a shine to Oscar.

"Monsieur Wilde," the fellow announced in response to a remark Oscar had intended as merely polite interest, "I shall escort you down the Eurydice mine, and you shall see –"

"See what...?" Oscar prompted.

"Nothing!" Antoine riposted with a giggle. "It is eternally dark down there."

"There is no flicker of light from the fires of Hell?"

"Not at this altitude, Monsieur. Not this high in the mountains."

Oscar tilted his head back and considered Antoine from under lowered lids. The fellow's bright, guileless expression did not falter, though Oscar was already certain that Antoine had the wit to be ironic.

"Come with me, s'il vous plait," Antoine pleaded. "It is not just tunnels and holes. We have broken through into a cavern truly wondrous. Such sculptures the Earth has created!"

"But I won't be able to see them."

Another giggle. "My friends and I, we will show you there with lanterns. And then, to see the eternal dark, we will leave you for a few minutes. We will withdraw, and then you will believe me. Not even the fires of Hell!"

An idea sparked in Oscar's mind. An elusive idea, that he chased without knowing why.

"But we won't go far, Monsieur. You will be perfectly safe. You will –"

What would he see in the dark? Oscar pondered the notion. What could he *only* see in the dark?

"I promise you, Monsieur, these sculptures are like nothing made by we humble creatures –"

Then it came to him, and he turned slightly away from Antoine's monologue, which hushed at last. There had been nights on his lecture tour when Oscar had woken late at night in his hotel room, and seen a glimmer of light that almost coalesced into... something. It had hovered on the edge of sight and then it would be gone, and he'd decided to dismiss it as moonlight glimpsing past the edge of the curtains, or candlelight creeping under the door. Every now and then, even during the day, sunlight or lamplight would glint off a surface unexpectedly, illogically. He'd known that practical explanations were inadequate – Not that he expected this to be the solution – However –

"I'll come," Oscar announced, "if you can bring me back in time for tea." He had managed to offend several of his American hosts and was conscious that not all of them had deserved it. "Merci, Antoine."

◆

They descended into the coolness of the Earth, down and farther down until Oscar felt dizzy with the sheer mass above his head. At last they reached the natural cavern, where Oscar was invited to sit on a convenient rock. Antoine deployed his five or six friends through the space, and they held up their lanterns to display pillars with ivory minerals rippling down the sides. Hanging sheets were made luminous with a lantern behind them, the light revealing streaks of brown and gold. A basin shone like an inverted pearl, into which water dropped at long intervals with a quiet *plunk*.

The cavern was indeed truly wondrous – but Oscar was there with another purpose. "Leave me now," he said to Antoine. "This is marvellous, but now I want to experience the dark."

"Are you sure, Monsieur?" Antoine asked in tones far more anxious than before.

"Yes, of course. You and your friends withdraw, as you planned –"

"No one wants to be left alone in the dark, Monsieur Wilde!"

"That is, however, why I came."

"Oscar, s'il vous plait, I shall stay with you, and my friends will return as soon as I call for them."

"I must insist, Antoine –"

"A minute or two only, then –"

"No," Oscar firmly replied. "I want you to leave me here for half an hour."

"Monsieur!" Antoine protested.

"There is something I can only achieve in the eternal dark."

The fellow was listening now, though he still appeared doubtful.

"Trust me," Oscar murmured for only the two of them to hear, "as I have trusted you."

The Earth punctuated this with a *plunk*.

"Oui, Monsieur," Antoine finally responded in kind. Then he was calling on his friends and herding them out of the cavern into the roughly hewn tunnels. Once they had gone, and the only light remaining was cast by Antoine's lantern, he came back to Oscar – and reached to clasp his hand. His skin was rough and precious and warm. "I will return for you." The most solemn of oaths. "I am sure you will not be frightened, Monsieur," Antoine continued, "but I will be frightened for you."

"Merci, Antoine," Oscar whispered – and when the man turned and walked away, Oscar closed his eyes and waited for the dark to descend.

◆

Plunk.

His eyes opened. Oscar had been half expecting to see nothing at all, for it to make no difference whether his eyes were closed or not. But then a slight gleam snagged his attention, and he turned towards it, and tried to focus on something that really shouldn't have been there.

Glowing lines defined the figure of a man, as if he were sketched upon the darkness itself. He sat carelessly on a boulder, not needing it for support but as if he were still in the habit of human behaviour. His head was propped on a hand, his elbow propped on a cocked knee, and he gazed off elsewhere, partly as if he could see their surroundings and partly as if he were contemplating more cerebral matters. More than that –

Oscar stirred a little and his spine lengthened, as he realised that the strong profile, the tumble of thick hair, and the short stature all reminded him of someone. "Mr Keats...?" he ventured.

The figure started, and looked about as if to find the source of this greeting. They both stared for a long moment before the other blurted out, "You can see me?"

"Yes! That is, only now, here, in the eternal darkness."

"One gets used to invisibility."

"Only the smallest glances before, that I dismissed as imagination."

"It is an odd kind of comfort, not to be observed."

Plunk.

As if recalled to the social niceties, the figure – whom Oscar must suppose to be the Ghost of John Keats – scrambled to stand. Perhaps his feet did not rest precisely on the ground. He bowed. "Mr Wilde. A pleasure."

Oscar would have stood as well, if he could see his immediate surroundings. The darkness made everything but the ghost unfathomable. Instead, he nodded with solemn dignity. "Mr Keats. The greatest of honours."

Keats huffed a laugh, looked away with a smile. "You are kind."

"Not always." Then he admitted, "Rarely."

Silence drifted them through several moments, and then Keats settled again on his rock.

Oscar asked, as polite as if in an English drawing room, "What brings you here, Mr Keats?"

"Why, *you* did, of course," Keats replied, as direct as if they were old friends.

Plunk.

"I visited – Rome," Oscar ventured, managing not to say 'your grave'. No doubt it was only natural that Keats' presence slowed Oscar's thoughts and sped his tongue.

"I remember," Keats said.

The spirit forbore to mention that Oscar had prostrated himself before that grave. "At least the cats were amused," Oscar remarked.

This amused Keats likewise. "*I gatti della Piramide a Roma...*" he murmured in passable

Italian – before continuing briskly, "They were fine companions, but it was then I decided to follow you here, to my brother's adopted country."

"Nonsense! I was in Rome four or five years ago, and the first I knew of this lecture tour was in September."

"Even so..."

Oscar pondered for a moment, but if ghosts or spirits were real and not merely the sort of thing one read about, then what else was possible? "You have a window, do you, with a view to the future?"

Keats shrugged, and gazed elsewhere.

Retreating to the metaphorical drawing room, Oscar asked, "You were with me in February, I trust, in Louisville, Kentucky, when I spent the day with your niece, Mrs Speed?"

"I was." After a while, Keats added, "I thank you."

Oscar nodded. It had been no hardship, after all. The former Miss Emma Frances Keats retained the sweet sharpness of youth, tempered by the calm of blameless maturity – and had inherited in full her father's love for the uncle she'd never met. Emma even looked rather like the poet – a comparison Oscar could now make with true authority.

"Did you ever wish you had to come to the New World yourself, with your brother?"

"No. There was much keeping me in England. My only wish was to remain there."

"Then you regret the last journey to Rome?"

Pain obscured the spirit's countenance.

"I do apologise," Oscar immediately offered. "I presume too much."

"I should have stayed," the spirit mused, "but my friends had hope, and insisted. I had none, and did not."

Oscar declared, "I think I could hold fast, with or without hope."

"Though all your friends urge otherwise?"

"Yes. Better to stand where you belong, and – " he reached for words and found a newly learnt phrase – "and face the music, whatever it might be."

Keats was pensive for timeless moments –

Plunk.

– but then regarded Oscar keenly. "Perhaps it's best not to decide now. Better to determine the course of action at the time. Listen to your friends."

"Though yours were wrong?"

"They were still worth listening to," the poet replied steadily.

Oscar equivocated, preferring to think that he already knew his own mind.

"It is never only you who is affected," Keats persisted. "Not only your friends and those you love – sometimes it is all the world."

Even Oscar felt this must be shameless exaggeration – and yet the spirit remained intent, which gave Oscar pause. "Are you looking through that window to the future or the past?" Oscar asked. "To mine or your own?"

The spirit did not answer, but turned his head away as if he had said enough.

"What if the world is wrong?" Oscar demanded.

Keats glanced at him, an empathetic spark of defiance glinting in his eyes. Perhaps he would agree that –

"Monsieur!"

Plunk.

For a moment the eternal dark surrounded Oscar and threatened to suffocate him – but then a glow off to one side announced the arrival of Antoine and his lantern. The man ran towards him, leaping nimbly from rock to rock, until at last he was there, carefully lowering his lantern to the ground – and then he was grasping Oscar's hand again, this time lifting it to press against his warm cheek.

"Monsieur, you are all right, tell me you are all right – the winch failed – we should never have retreated so far, but you wanted to know the true darkness –"

"I am well, my friend," he reassured the fellow, reaching his other hand to firmly clasp Antoine's shoulder.

"It has been longer than half an hour – *far* longer – I feared the worst –"

"I had no idea of the time passing, but I do not mind at all. It has been... illuminating."

"Monsieur," Antoine whispered, before shifting to bless Oscar's hand with a kiss.

There were footsteps barely discernible in the distance, and a confusion of voices. "Fie on faint hearts!" Oscar muttered – and he slid his other hand around Antoine's nape, drawing him close while leaning in to kiss the man on the mouth.

They embraced hungrily, and only parted as company drew nigh. "Tonight, monsieur?" Antoine dared to suggest.

"Tonight," Oscar agreed. He knew his own nature, for certain sure — and he knew the world was wrong.

◆

Chooser of the Slain

◆

In the middle of winter, just past the solstice as the world turned slowly back towards the light, Lily picked her way across the mud of a ruined field in France. Men had emerged from the trenches on either side, and now stood there together, talking or miming their shared goodwill, and exchanging what modest gifts they had to hand. Others played a ball game, not one force against the other but all nationalities and all ranks intermingled. None of them saw her.

There was only one figure in that field who knew Lily was there. A Valkyrie stood over a corpse sprawled midway between the trenches; her head was bowed, her helmet tucked under her arm and her sword was sheathed. She looked fine and fierce. After a while Lily joined her there, and they stood beside each other, sharing a long moment of silent respect for the dead man's courage and sacrifice.

Then the Valkyrie lifted her head and looked across at Lily. "Have you chosen him, then?"

"Perhaps," she replied. "I haven't yet decided."

"His grandame was from Hamburg, and he was named for her father."

"Yes. But he was born in Colchester and fought for Britain."

They fell quiet again. The soldiers had already recovered the few wounded who'd been stranded in range of the enemy; now they began recovering what remained of the dead, and carrying them back behind the trenches, some to one side and some to the other.

The Valkyrie watched for a time, her attention drawn towards the other fallen from whom she might choose, as they were taken towards the fields on the east. Eventually she turned back towards Lily. "I'm Kara," she said, offering her right hand.

"Lily," she replied, clasping that hand in hers for a moment.

"If I choose this one, Lily, I will take him to Valhalla, a great golden hall presided over by the god Odin."

"And if I choose him, Kara, he will sleep with the great king Arthur and his knights, until Britain has need of them again."

Kara nodded. "He will be glad to be of use once more – and he *will* be of use, as Odin prepares him and his fellow warriors for the great catastrophe of Ragnarök."

Lily tilted her head, acknowledging the point. Ragnarök threatened the whole world, and anyone who loved what was good would be proud to work against it.

"Meanwhile," Kara continued, "he will live in a man's idea of paradise: a hall of many pillars, rooved with golden shields and great spears for rafters – and my sisters serving him mead never-ending."

"I would give him rest," Lily countered. "He would feast on wild honey, and then lie down garlanded with flowers on a greensward gently rising beside a quiet lake. They sleep undisturbed. Even their dreams are kind." She sighed. "Where else in life or death could he find such perfect peace?"

It was Kara's turn to acknowledge an excellent point well made.

"I give them peace – and they declare I am without mercy," Lily continued with a hint of bitterness. "They blame me for being beautiful, when it is them who find me so. I only appear as I am, and they make of that what they will – not what I will. I sing them to rest, and they think I am casting a spell!"

"The fallen are afraid," Kara responded. "The fear distorts their understanding."

Lily huffed a breath, her impatience turning ironic the more she considered the matter. "Yes – I offer them peace, but they are quite naturally afraid of the unknown."

After a moment, Kara suggested, "It is that poet's fault. Poets are rarely our friends – don't you find, La Belle Dame?"

A slightly wicked smile grew on Lily's lips. "Ah yes, that poet. I chose him, Kara," she confessed. "He died too young, though not in battle. He was... quite surprised when he knew me. But we talked long over the honey and the manna, and I believe he understood before he slipped away to sleep; he'd had so little peace in life. And Arthur will have need of poets, too."

Kara was watching her with eyes aglow, and when Lily had finished her tale she said, "You did well, sister."

Lily nodded her thanks. "So," she said, indicating the man by whom they stood. "Is this one for Odin or for Arthur?"

"I am loath for either of us to take him, Lily. I would not have anyone say that we disputed and that one of us lost."

"What shall we do, then?"

"Let us leave him for Freyja instead. He will be happy there, in her hall Sessrúmnir, amidst a beautiful sea of meadows."

They clasped hands again in agreement, and then each looked to where the last of the corpses were being stretchered away from no man's land. There was work to be done.

"So many fallen..." Kara whispered. "Odin and Freyja will welcome them, but even the gods mourn at times such as these."

"That is so," Lily agreed, peering across leagues to where an ambulance had driven over a mine in the road. "Well, Arthur will be glad of these nurses, too. Their blood was as fierce as any other's here."

"Fare thee well, sister," Kara cried, as she rose into the air.

"Fare thee well!"

◆

Misplaced

♦

The town of Reading, Berkshire dated back at least to Saxon times, if not Roman times, with records confirming a ninth-century settlement at the crossing of the River Kennet, a little way upstream from where it joined the Thames. Not that Sam expected to find anything dating back so far; a thousand years after that settlement was established, the Victorians industriously overlaid almost everything but the old abbey ruins. Still, she was enjoying the chance to poke around in what was being uncovered by the wholescale redevelopment of the Reading railway station. Like many children, she'd dreamed about being an archaeologist. Sometimes, working as an engineer in this land with its long history was the next best thing.

She lived in Slough – so would often take a train back to Reading on a day off, don a hardhat, grab a torch, and wave her security pass before slipping through an Authorised Personnel Only door and going exploring.

That day, Sam was heading for an area recently unearthed below what had been the old station's cellar. There were three rooms that led from one to the other. It had been declared safe, insofar as no one expected it all to collapse, but Sam couldn't deny it felt as if the space had been ramshackle even in its heyday. This wasn't helped by the fact that natural light had found its way down through cracks and crevices into the farthest room. Which meant that plenty of rain had probably poured through over the years, too, though it seemed to have also drained away efficiently, if more by luck than good management.

Sam spent a short while examining the jagged gap about fifteen inches wide where the ceiling met the south wall, aiming her torch at it from various angles, and made a note to herself to find the hole on the surface and have it filled in. There didn't seem to be anything much of interest otherwise.

But as she was about to leave, Sam realised that there was something she'd missed. Her torchlight had swept across the north wall where, obscured by dimness and dust, there were shelves set into an alcove. And the shelves appeared to be stacked with old boxes. She couldn't see much in situ, so she carefully eased one out of hiding, and lowered it to the floor. The box itself seemed ready to fall apart, but she gently lifted out the top object. A manila folder thickly layered in dust, containing paperwork that seemed to relate to station business. It was difficult to make out the details of the faded ink and foxed paper. Not very exciting, even if it dated back to the mid-1800s, but worth preserving and having a look at. The local museum or library might find something of interest. A second box contained more files and blank stationery.

Sam was just about to give up for the weekend and return on Monday in an official capacity, when she noticed something poking up out of another box that wasn't just paperwork. She was quite short, and it was hard to reach up far enough, but she managed to tease the box forward enough for it to fall into her arms – at which point the box disintegrated and everything fell through her hold onto the floor... except for an old leather briefcase.

She stood there for a long moment, staring down at it. One corner of it was particularly dry and hardened, so that must have been what caught her attention. The rest of it seemed to prove it well used in its time, but also relatively well preserved since. And it was heavy, as if it might contain something of interest. Sam spun about to face the natural light that filtered through, and folded down to sit cross-legged on the floor, planting the torch beside her.

The case's clasps were stiff, but she managed to wrestle them open. Inside was a ream or two of used paper. Sam carefully slid it out and riffled through the top left corner. It seemed every page was dense with typewriting and handwritten notes; the ink of the notes was faded, and the edges of the pages were discoloured, but the typed characters seemed as bold and brisk as the day they were made.

She returned to the first page and read a handwritten note – 'Where to start! Latest moment possible and finish at the earliest.' – and then the typewritten title – 'Revolt in the Desert'. There was no byline. For a long moment she sat there staring at the words as thoughts and vague memories realigned... Then...

"Holy fuck," Sam whispered. Could this

possibly be the manuscript of Lawrence of Arabia's *Seven Pillars of Wisdom*, supposedly lost almost a century ago while the author was changing trains on his way to Oxford?

She almost put it down in a state of overwhelm, but then became aware that something had changed, there was more light, or – a presence maybe – Sam's instinctive reaction was to clutch the precious manuscript to her chest. With a catch in her voice, she demanded, "Who's there?"

"I believe you know," came a dusty murmur. Then a sigh. "Doesn't everyone, still?"

The light from the gap in the ceiling had formed into a beam, and then as Sam watched a shadow emerged and became a human shape and then solidified. A lean man, not much taller than Sam herself, dressed casually in what might have been old military rejects. "Lawrence," she ventured.

"Shaw," he countered.

Sam grinned. "It *is* you." Who cared if he had died seventy-some years before? Sam patted the manuscript held safe in her embrace. "Some of your friends thought this had been stolen. Deliberately, I mean. Like, an intelligence operation."

The ghost stuck his hands into his trouser pockets and shrugged. "Nonsense. Hardly worth the effort."

"You weren't... indiscreet, then?"

"They would have been more worried about my notes."

"Which you burnt. As you wrote this."

A sceptical eyebrow cocked, and he seemed almost real now. Solid, though still bathed in sunlight. "You suggest that this was the only remaining record of... certain matters?"

"Exactly."

"Ha!" Lawrence scoffed. "A Boy's Own adventure in the desert."

Sam wasn't fooled. "You know *Seven Pillars* was so much more than that."

He shifted, as if wanting to change tack. "An adventure –"

"It was *everything* to me," Sam insisted. "It helped me know myself."

Lawrence's brow lifted in doubt, but it seemed that despite himself he wanted to hear more.

Sam continued, "You've heard the saying 'A square peg in a round hole', yes?"

"Yes."

"Well, you were always more like a seven-sided peg in a round hole."

"Heptagon," he commented distantly, before his attention snapped back to Sam. "A seven-sided polygon is a heptagon."

"Yes. Anyway. That's why I liked you. I was assigned male at birth, see, and –"

"Assigned male," the ghost echoed, seeming taken aback. "As was I."

"Yes, and that's, like, the one thing you never questioned or challenged, am I right?"

"Yes..." After a moment he added more firmly, "For myself, yes." Then, a little gentler, "I knew of men and women who did question such things, though."

"Because of them, we get to choose now. We get to live it."

Lawrence nodded thoughtfully. "A few of them lived it... or tried to."

"They were brave." Sam sighed, and remarked, "You still need to be brave, though. Even today."

A silence stretched, before the ghost gathered himself. "I am failing to see the connection. Nevertheless, Ms Samantha –"

"How did you –?" She scrambled to her feet.

The light grew stronger, as did his tone. "I would appreciate you putting the manuscript down and moving aside."

Sam hugged the papers close. "No – Why?"

"Do as I say, please." He was used to command, he was used to convincing people, and the sunlight seemed to robe him in Arabian white. Did that add to his authority? "*Now*."

Slowly she did as he willed, at last bending to place the manuscript on its briefcase, and then straightening up again. They both considered it. "Are you sure?" she whispered.

"It was never meant for others, but only as a place to start for myself." After a moment he added, "Step away, if you would."

Sam barely took a step or two backwards, for the conflagration was narrowly focused. The light flared and then focussed, as if Lawrence held a magnifying glass, and then the pages were alight. They burned with an odd, localised intensity, and then even the ashes fell into grey dust, as if the fire had taken place back in 1919 when the manuscript was left behind.

But what had she given up? Why hadn't she –? "Colonel Lawrence," Sam began. She could have held on to this precious piece of history and run out of there... Had it even been the author's decision to make?

"Thank you, Ms Samantha," was the only reply.

Why hadn't she... Why hadn't she... When she looked up again, the light had already dwindled back to what it had been, and there was no Lawrence, and nothing at her feet – but for a ragged old case – that proved she had held what she'd held.

In the end I agreed, she reflected; *and then at once I knew how much I was sorry.*

◆

We Live Without a Future

◆

The sitting room on the ground floor was placed low, snugly nestled into the ground, and it was luminous and green with living light. At times it seemed as if it were all one with the garden, the Monk's House garden tended with ruthless beneficence by Leonard. At other times the living room seemed as if it were a peaceful dell of water, hidden far beneath the bright surface flow of the river.

In times past the room had seemed the quietest of refuges. Now it was piled about with the books they had rescued from the wreckage of the house in Mecklenburgh Square. And no matter how often Virginia wiped and scrubbed at the books, they seemed always smothered in the black soft dust left behind by the bombing.

Was it cowardly to admit, Virginia wondered, that she had been pleased to be forced to abandon their home in London? She had always felt that all of life was to be found in London, and yet now – perhaps she was growing old – the quietness of Rodmell village, steeped in Sussex rusticity, induced a long trance of pleasure. Even the Messerschmitt aeroplane that had been shot down nearby looked like nothing more than a moth that had settled with its wings extended on the grassy slope of Mount Caburn.

There were days and days of nothing but peace, freedom, just Leonard and Virginia doing for themselves, and reading and writing and corresponding, and biting into the crisp luxury of pears from the garden with the juice running down their chins.

Then another plane would grind low overhead, with a humming and a sawing and a buzzing that was so loud it vibrated through her very marrow. If she and Leonard were out walking, they would hide under a tree or at the edge of a haystack, lying face-down with arms sheltering their heads. "I don't want to die yet," Virginia said to Leonard. Though there was something fine and clean about the idea of Leonard and Virginia – the Wolves, as she liked to call them – standing tall and fierce, hand in hand in the open, and being broken together.

The bombs dropped – some as near as Lewes – but never quite found them at Rodmell. It seemed only a matter of time. And if not the bombs, then the German invasion, which was always to happen in the next week or two, or maybe the week after that. Shipping was massing at French ports, the Channel had never seemed narrower, and of course the air raids were only a Prologue to make the English cower, and Act One would open with the German troops landing at Eastbourne. The last time that England was successfully invaded, Virginia mused, was so long ago that the landing place at Pevensey was now a mile inland, and so that wouldn't do at all.

It seemed almost fated. Although in

September a gale rose and England was saved once more by Armada weather. Despite which, the invasion still seemed inevitable.

The Wolves' group of friends had mostly survived the Great War, and the Spanish War – though they had lost Julian in Spain, and Nessa was for ever changed by a mother's grief for her favourite son – but now this was too much. Not only the air raids, the bombs, the ghastly stories and rumours one heard... It was all another step beyond anything reasonable, anything that could be understood, that could be survived.

Before the rationing made it impossible, Leonard had stowed a full can of petrol in the garage. That was to be their end: going to sleep in the car, perhaps even at midday if it became necessary, with Leonard reading to her, his beloved measured voice reading to her, so that she need not focus on the untimely darkness nor the rumble of the engine.

What made it necessary for him was that Leonard was a Jew. What made it necessary for her was that Virginia could not live at all comfortably without him, not any more. She would fall into madness again, and with Leonard gone there would be no one to catch her. Not even Vanessa could care for her as Leonard did. And it was said time and again that the invaders would force the subjugated to give up their Jews, and so it would not only be the Germans coming for Leonard, but the English pointing the way. How could they want to live?

Vita visited from Sissinghurst in February, and said that she and Harold had made plans likewise. They each had a lethal pill, which Harold called a 'bare bodkin'. Vita took it from her handbag, to show Virginia, and they peered at it together.

"Harold knows he's been too outspoken, you see," Vita explained as she put the pill away. "Well, just as outspoken as he should be, for us – but too loud on the wrong side of the question for Herr Hitler." She gave the title mockingly, and then leaned near Virginia again to say with sincerity, "You and Leonard, too, of course. You've both made your views plain on this fascist nightmare Germany has succumbed to. But not me!" Vita laughed lightly. "I am sure they neither know nor care that I exist – but then Harold says there'll be much I'd rather avoid. Who wants to be occupied? The pain, the humiliation... not to mention the sheer tedium."

Vita laughed again, and Virginia could hardly help but smile despite the topic. "It isn't only the politics," Virginia said, "but that Leonard is a Jew."

A pat on the hand from Vita. "I do remember, my darling!"

"And all our friends..." They were on the sofa in the upstairs sitting room, drinking tea, and now Virginia put down her cup and lay back to rest her head, unable to support the thought. "I cannot imagine that any one of us will not be in danger. Except perhaps Vanessa, though she'll be tainted by association, and I suppose they will not like her living apart from Clive. But think of our men! A good half of them are buggers, and the Nazis despise homosexuals."

"I know," said Vita with a sympathetic sigh.

"Did you ever talk with Isherwood? Morgan's friend?" That wild boy Isherwood, just a slip of a thing with quicksilver eyes. He had been forced to leave Berlin in 1933 when Hitler and the Nazi party came into power. It had been quite the haven until then. There had been a growing sense of freedom, real freedom. "If even half the boy's tales are true –"

"I know, I know. Arrests. Interrogations. Concentration camps. Death." Vita paused, before saying in straightforward tones, "The latter does seem preferable, if a choice must be made."

Virginia also sighed, still musing on Isherwood. As the war loomed, he had travelled to America and comparative safety. Some accused him of running away, but after what he had seen in Berlin, one could hardly blame him for wanting to escape.

"You're thinking…" Vita began, her hand pushing closer to Virginia's where it lay on the sofa seat. "You're thinking that Herr Hitler will not like Sapphists, either, nor feminists."

Virginia turned her head to consider Vita, and let the assumption stand.

Vita continued tartly, "Nor anyone who's ready, willing and able to speak against him. What hope do any of us have?" Then she put down her empty cup, and patted the sofa cushion between them so that Virginia felt the slight vibration of it ripple through her. "Now, my lively little squirrel," Vita said, "come nearer and nestle."

And Virginia wanted nothing more in all the world than to nestle with this enchantress – but a slight archness in Vita's tone made her bristle, a slight smugness and a coquettish smile made Virginia feel ignorant and dowdy, when moments before she would have happily sunk into that offered embrace and never surfaced till morning. Was it Vita's occasional cluelessness or Virginia's nervousness most to blame?

"Oh, no," Vita murmured sorrowfully. "Now I've made you skittish."

Virginia huffed irritably – but rather than let that ruin this chance of a cuddle, she took a deep breath and dived in closer to Vita, and somehow in the woman's arms she transformed from a sharp-elbowed scarecrow to something supple and strong. Vita slowly, deliciously edged closer – surreptitiously, as if it weren't utterly obvious what she was about – until at last she stole a kiss, and they communed directly, honestly, mouth to mouth. For a few moments Virginia felt a tidal surge of passion deep below...

...but then it gently ebbed away again, and the two of them settled into a warm bundle that contained all the perfections that Virginia had ever craved.

Leonard found them like that some while later, when he came in from the garden, the soil still darkening the whorls of his finger-pads. He grunted a greeting, completely unsurprised. "We have more leeks growing than will ever be wanted at Lewes market. Do you want to take some home with you, Vita?"

"That would be marvellous, Leonard, thank you," Vita replied warmly, smoothly, not shifting her hold on his wife, nor reminding him of the bounteous gardens at Sissinghurst.

"Good." For a moment, Leonard's piercing blue gaze considered Virginia, but then when he had satisfied himself that she was as happy as she might be, he turned away muttering, "Letters to answer." A moment later he was in his study, quietly closing the door behind him to give them privacy.

A still moment passed, and then Vita gently asked, "How are you *really*, my darling?"

Virginia sighed... and resisted the urge to tense up into her regular posture. "Don't let's spoil things, dearest."

And Vita pressed a kiss to Virginia's hair, and let all the dreary things be. The peace lasted all the afternoon, and all evening, and when Virginia lay down that night alone in her narrow bed, she slept as soundly as if there were no such things as dreams.

Vita left the next day, though, and despite all Leonard's tenderly firm care of Virginia, she grew restless again. There was *Between the Acts* to rescue from mediocrity, if she possibly could, but she could not concentrate, could not even quiet her mind enough to read something entirely unrelated. Not that revising her work was ever easy, but the task felt particularly freighted now, the heaviest of the many things weighing her down.

Neither did it help that the birds began mocking her whenever she walked down through the garden to her writing lodge. "Skimble-skamble," one squawked. "Skimble-skamble."

The water meadows stretched from the foot of their garden away into the hazy distance, peacefully gleaming under the cool clear sunshine.

"Nothing's solid!" another bird shrieked.

"Very solid or very shifting?" quibbled its mate.

"Nothing's solid!"

"What's the Channel?" chirped another. "What's the Channel, if they mean to invade us? What's the Channel?"

And if Virginia couldn't settle, then poor Leonard couldn't settle either, and he couldn't work, not properly. Not that he ever complained, but the world was darker without the light of his formidable intellect shining upon it, while it could do very well without a trivial novel about a village play.

"Orts, scraps and fragments!" the neighbour's chickens clucked. "Orts, scraps and fragments!"

Eventually, inevitably, it all narrowed down to only one solution. She had tried it before, but this time she would succeed. She owed it to herself to succeed. And Leonard would be stronger without her distractions, and somehow it seemed possible that England would be stronger, too, that England might stand firm against the forces ranged against it, if only it could be sure of this fiercely intelligent Jew standing firm on English soil, staring across the sea at the Continent. He might have his hands in his pockets, but his stature was unbending, and his sharp blue eyes saw through everything. That was enough. That was more than enough. And she was just getting in the way.

"The wheels scurred on the gravel... the wheels scurred... scurred... the wheels scurred."

Each stone that she put into her coat pockets lightened her burdens, and then the river welcomed her down into its darkness, and the salt water promised her rest in the endless peaceful energy of the ocean. True, she struggled for long painful moments – but she struggled against the struggle – and her will was stronger, and she calmed again.

Virginia drifted past...

◆ ◆ ◆

About the Author

♦

Ordinary people are extraordinary. We can all aspire to decency, generosity, respect, honesty – and the power of love (all kinds of love!) can help us grow into our best selves.

I write stories about 'ordinary' people finding their answers in themselves and each other. I write about friends and lovers, and the families we create for ourselves. I explore the depth and the meaning, the fun and the possibilities, in 'everyday' experiences and relationships. I believe that embodying these things is how we can live our lives more fully.

Creative works help us each find our own clarity and our own joy. Readers bring their hearts and souls to reading, just as authors bring their hearts and souls to writing – and together we make a whole.

I read books, lots of books, and watch films. I admire art, and love theatre and music. I try to be an awesome partner, sister, friend. I live an engaged and examined life. And I strive to write as honestly as I can.

I have lived in two countries – England and Australia – which has helped widen my perspective, and I have travelled as well. I love learning, and have completed courses in all kinds of things. My careers have been in Human Resources, and in eLearning and training, so there has always been a focus on my fellow human beings and on understanding, conveying, sharing information.

Knitting gives me some down time and the chance to craft something with my hands. Coffee gives me stimulation and a certain street cred. My favourite colour has segued from pure blue to dark purple, and now to teal and other greeny blues.

I think John Keats is the best person who has ever lived.

And that's me!

Julie Bozza. Quirky. Queer. Sincere.

Website: **juliebozza.com**

◆

Titles by Julie Bozza

◆

The Butterfly Hunter Trilogy:
    Butterfly Hunter
    Of Dreams and Ceremonies
    Like Leaves to a Tree (story)
    The Thousand Smiles of Nicholas Goring

Novels and Novellas:
    The Apothecary's Garden
    The Definitive Albert J. Sterne
    The Fine Point of His Soul
    Homosapien ... a fantasy about pro wrestling

Mitch Rebecki Gets a Life
A Night with the Knight of the Burning Pestle
A Threefold Cord
The 'True Love' Solution
The Valley of the Shadow of Death
Writ in Blood

Stories and Anthologies:
Call to Arms
A Certain Persuasion
Clarity
Crisis at Christmas & Christmas Present
A Death in Tombstone, A.T.
An English Heaven
Geek Elders Speak
Heroines
Love in Every Stitch
No Holds Bard
No Man's Land
A Pride of Poppies
Queer Weird West Tales
Rock Paper Water
Wyngraf

Translations:
Chasseur de papillons (French)
La cérémonie (French)
Les mille sourires de Nicholas Goring
   (French)
Nous (French)
Jäger des verlorenen Schmetterlings
   (German)

www.ingramcontent.com/pod-product-compliance
Lightning Source LLC
Chambersburg PA
CBHW060749210726
48292CB00015B/2878